Sir Parsley and the Dragon

and Other Stories

For Olivia,
my little dragon

ISBN 978-1-84753-439-2

Contents

Sir Parsley and the Dragon

By Crumley Bridge on Pigton Moor,
there lived a mighty knight,
He rode a spotty charger,
and his singular delight,
was hunting dragons big or small,
he didn't care a whit,
He didn't care for scaly monsters,
not a tiny bit.

The knight had many names among
the people of the moors,
They called him their protector,
and they opened up their doors,
To welcome brave Sir Parsley,
for such was his given name,
And offer him assistance,
as he played his deadly game.

Above the moors there stood a mountain,
soaring to the skies,
And on the other side,
there was a cave of wondrous size,
Where hid a dragon, huge and red,
reclining on its treasure,
The knight was sure it contemplated
evil without measure.

When late one evening, in the gloom
the massive beast descended,
on Crumley Bridge on Pigton Moor,
the townsfolk were offended,
They called for Parsley,
hoping he could stop the beast returning,
and offer them some respite,
for their fields were black and burning.

Sir Parsley took the job with pride
and on his spotty steed,
He rode up to the mountain
to perform his hero's deed,
The mountainside was craggy,
but the knight was not deterred,
he quickly reached the cave
where dragon snoring could be heard.

The dragon softly slumbered
on a tumbled hoard of gold,
The treasure was invaluable,
a wonder to behold.
The dragon's tail flicked slowly
as the monster dreamed and twitched,
and pawed the cavern floor
as if its body was bewitched.

Sir Parsley slowly walked
to where the dragon lay at rest,
He picked his way through piles of treasure,
past a wooden chest.
The dragon snorted loudly
and blew smoke out of its nose,
Sir Parsley coughed and spluttered,
but the beast remained adoze.

Sir Parsley crept up closer still
and poked the monster's bum,
It opened up one bleary eye
and bared a toothy gum,
It rounded on Sir Parsley
and it peered down at the knight,
And opened up it's mighty mouth
and gave the man a fright.

Sir Parsley was no coward,
but the dragon's teeth were vast,
Pointy, white and wicked sharp,
the knight was quite aghast,
He backed away until he found
his back against the wall,
and fervently he prayed and wished
he wasn't there at all.

"What have I done to you, Sir knight,
that you prod me this way?"
The dragon cocked its head
and flicked its tail in dismay,
"I don't come into your home,
and proceed to poke your bottom",
"I can't see how I've done you harm,
unless I've quite forgotten"

Sir Parsley was surprised
to be addressed in such a manner,
Dragons mostly ate his lance
or set alight his banner,
They generally weren't disposed
to civil conversation,
And certainly did not respond
with fuddled indignation.

The dragon shuffled round a bit
to get a better look,
At the proud and haughty knight
intent on going by the book,
The book said "dragons do not talk"
and "dragons eat your kids"
And "dragons are capricious beasts,
we really should get rid".

The book, in this case,
was completely wrong in every way,
For dragons come in many forms,
too numerous to say,
Among them are the nasty beasts
of which we have just heard,
But there are those that wouldn't
harm a flea or little bird.

Sir Parsley was a gallant man,
but not overly bright,
In short he had the makings of
a truly special knight,
A sword arm like a tree trunk
and a sure hand on the reins,
But for all that,
the man was just a little short on brains.

He swung hard at the dragon,
it was all he knew to do,
The dragon dodged and parried
as he tried to run it through,
But the dragon waned and tired
and before long couldn't fight,
And it hung its head and pleaded
for the mercy of the knight.

Sir Parsley raised his sword aloft
to strike the creature down,
"Sir knight, I pray you, have a heart,
I never burned the town,
I stole the civic jewelry,
but I never touched the people,
I only took the mayor's gold
and cherub from the steeple."

"I don't converse with monsters,"
said the brave and noble knight,
"I'll see to it that you can't cause
another dose of fright"
He swung his mighty sword down hard
upon the dragon's throat,
The massive head was severed
as the beast was duly smote.

Sir Parsley stood above the dragon's
broken, battered shell,
and thought he spied a movement
by the old town church's bell,
There lay an egg upon the ground,
its surface chipped and cracked,
So much in disarray
that an inhabitant it lacked.

Amidst the dragon's hoard
Sir Parsley saw a lick of flame,
And when he saw the source of it,
it filled him through with shame,
For by the pile of gilded knicknacks
stood a lonely shape,
A little dragon, small enough
to fit in Parsley's cape.

At once Sir Parsley saw the cause
of all the township's woes,
As the dragon breathed upon the treasure,
brave Sir Parsley froze,
The dragon lapped up molten gold
like milk spilt from a jug,
And Parsley hung his head in shame,
he felt like such a mug.

The dragon stole the civic gold
to feed it's tiny offspring,
It didn't really care at all
about inflicting suffering,
Its only plan was getting hold
of lots and lots of gold,
To feed the tiny infant
who was barely minutes old.

Sir Parsley really was a knight
and noble through and through,
So right there on the spot
our hero knew just what to do,
He wrapped the little dragon
in his flowing crimson cape,
And from the mother dragon's lair
the pair made their escape.

They went down to the town
and Parsley tried to tell the tale,
But no one there would have it,
they thought he'd been at the ale,
They called him names and ridiculed
the story he had told them,
And asked him where their money was
and all their treasures golden.

Sir Parsley felt a pang of guilt
for stashed about his person,
Was plenty gold to keep the dragon
fed a year for certain,
He got back on his charger
and he left town in disgrace,
The mayor firmly told him
nevermore to show his face.

The dragon and the noble knight
went back out on the moor,
And made themselves at home there,
though their hut was rather poor,
They lived a quiet life
for several years there all alone,
The dragon and the knight were bonded,
right down to the bone.

In time the dragon learned to speak,
and Parsley's life was full,
Of dragon-banter, dragon-wit
and nothing dragon-dull,
Sir Parsley was as happy
as he ever hoped to be,
And the dragon grew up big and strong
and was a sight to see.

One day the dragon went to hunt,
and nevermore returned,
The knight was quite distraught,
the mighty heart within him burned,
He searched the moors in desperation,
but couldn't find a thing,
Not a tooth or claw or whisker,
nor a scale or tail or wing.

Sir Parsley mourned alone
upon the moors outside the town,
His grief was such the sun
was only ever going down,
The mighty knight was broken
and he let his body go,
Until he was a shell of what
the townsfolk used to know.

Our hero was a sorry state
when one day in the tavern,
He heard about a mighty beast
some boys caught in a cavern,
They locked it up at once
inside the dusty, draughty jail,
And Parsley hoped that just for once
true justice might prevail.

But it seemed the people weren't content
with locking up the beast,
They wanted blood and torment
and they planned a mighty feast,
They'd kill the monster, then adjourn
to dinner and a dance,
Our hero simply could not permit
such a circumstance.

The grizzled man who told the tale
bade Parsley hold his tongue,
For, it seems, the fellow's
horrid story wasn't done,
The jail cell was empty
when they came again next morn,
Except for a girl, with golden hair,
lost and all forlorn.

They let the lady out at once,
but no one could agree,
On what had happened to the beast,
for it was plain to see,
That somehow the creature had escaped
and fled to whence it came,
To bring again its wrath upon the town
with claw and flame.

"Flame?" said Parsley, "Is it true?
A dragon in the town?"
"Aye," said the man, "a dragon true,
and fit to burn it down!"
"This past few weeks we've had no sleep,
nor rest from all our fear,"
"For if the dragon comes again,
it's sure to cost us dear.

Just then a man burst through the door,
his face was ghastly white,
Parsley didn't need an explanation
for his fright,
He leapt up from the table
and he sprinted out the door,
The man had seen a dragon,
of that Parsley was quite sure.

And sure enough as Parsley looked
across the moors he saw,
A massive beast about to give
the townspeople what for,
It hovered like a stately, scaly
butterfly in flight,
But for Parsley it was not
an altogether awful sight.

For he had hopes it was his friend,
that he had raised from birth,
So Parsley took his charger
and rode for all that he was worth,
Towards the town like lightning
streaked the knight upon his steed,
Upon the beast's behalf our hero
dearly wished to plead.

But as he neared the town
he plainly saw to his dismay,
It wasn't his friend dragon
about to join the fray,
This monster was another kind
of dragon altogether,
Its scales were black and horny
and its hide looked tough as leather.

The beast aimed for the people
with a jet of golden flame,
And Sir Parsley rode to once again
resume his deadly game,
For this was no good dragon,
forced to steal to feed its brood,
But an evil-minded brute with thoughts
of nothing more than food.

Sir Parsley closed upon the beast,
his lance was at the ready,
His arm was locked like iron
as he held the weapon steady,
But though he struck the dragon true,
the lance just glanced away,
And Sir Parsley fled the dragon's breath
and kept its teeth at bay.

He wheeled round for another charge,
but halted as he saw,
A lovely girl with golden hair
come to him across the moor,
She said, "Sir knight, you'll lose this fight,
if you don't take my aid"
"Come fly with me and you will see,
we'll make this beast afraid"

The lady stopped in front of him
and changed before his eyes,
Her arms grew long and scaly
and she quadrupled in size,
Her back grew wings, her neck grew long
and presently he found,
His old friend stood before him,
gently pawing at the ground.

"Come fly on me, and you will find
we'll beat this monster back"
"Your arm is true and powerful,
but altitude you lack"
"I'll fly with you, old friend," said Parsley,
"gladly that I will"
He drunk the dragon's presence in
until he'd had his fill.

He swung himself behind the wings
of his enormous steed,
And flew into the sky
content to take the dragon's lead,
She wheeled about and found
the other creature swooping low,
Over Crumley Bridge on Pigton Moor
intent on causing woe.

Sir Parsley raised his lance anew
and down the pair careered,
Like a slender silver arrow,
sent to see the monster speared,
Sir Parsley locked his arm in place
and this time made his mark,
The beast was down, upon the ground,
its scarlet eyes were dark.

Our noble knight dismounted now,
and pleaded with his friend,
"Please be again the girl I saw,
and make my misery end",
"For truly you're more beautiful
than anything I've seen",
"Would that I were a king,
that I might make you my queen"

The dragon changed to girl again,
and took Sir Parsley's hand,
And by the grin upon her face,
it's sure that this she planned,
She planted such a kiss
upon our hero's startled face,
That his knees were turned to water
and his heart began to race.

In time the pair were married,
and no happier knight you'll see,
Than Parsley, lord of Dragonhame,
where dragons wander free,
And no happier dragon in the land
than Peregrin, his mate,
Who knows she owes her world
to noble honour, love and fate.

The Dream Peddler

In ages past and times gone by,
when all the world was new,
There lived a bent and wizened man,
Whose name was Pongo Foo,
He walked the thin and cobbled streets
in boots of beetle leather,
And in his hair, applied with care,
he wore an ostrich feather.

His battered coat was rhino hide,
his gloves were Irish Setter.
In knowledge gen'ral all agreed
he had no peer nor better,
No, Pongo Foo was no mere man,
no fool like you or I,
He knew the names of all the ants,
and how the pigeons fly.

Old Pongo was a peddler,
and jack of many trades,
But the one that he loved best
was selling weavings that he made.
These trinkets weren't just gaudy baubles,
ornaments and things,
They told a tale and wove a dream
with all that fancy brings.

He made them out of finest silk,
in strands of silver-gold,
In patterns that would tease the eye
and let the tale take hold,
He sold them on the narrow streets
to little girls and boys,
Who took them home and hung them up,
or stashed them with their toys.

And when the night time came at last,
and quiet darkness fell,
The trifles worked their magic,
and dispensed dreams for a spell.
For when the children peered at them,
and tried to trace the thread,
Their eyes would gently close
and they would snuggle up in bed.

The children dreamed of wondrous dragons,
witches, knights and thieves,
They settled under gilded trees
and counted golden leaves,
They spent their nights in wonderment
at Pongo's fine creation,
A spool of thread, a magic spell,
a child's imagination.

Now in those days, and in that place,
there lived a lad called Jack,
Who'd visit Pongo every day
to rummage in his sack,
One sunny morning Jack awoke,
and wandered to the square,
But Pongo Foo could not be found,
he simply wasn't there.

Young Jack looked hard around the town
for traces of his friend,
He looked in every alleyway,
and even round the bend,
But Pongo still eluded him,
he'd vanished from the scene,
Until he asked the market master,
Aloysius Green.

The market master told the lad
that Pongo Foo was ill,
He'd stayed at home in bed
to ease the symptoms of his chill,
Jack asked him for his friend's address
and this the master gave,
Along with an admonishment
to be kind and behave.

"He doesn't need a little boy
to trouble him with nonsense",
"He needs some rest, don't be a pest,
or be it on your conscience!"
Jack heeded Mr. Green's advice,
and promised to be good,
He'd simply sit by Pongo's side
and help him if he could.

He found the place with ease enough,
it wasn't very hard,
There aren't too many houses
with a tiger in the yard.
He knocked on Pongo's door
and heard the peddler cough, "Come in!"
Old Pongo lay upon the bed,
pale of face and thin.

"Come closer, lad, It's not contagious",
Pongo Foo proclaimed,
"I'm not unwell, just tired.
It's old age that's to be blamed."
Jack didn't like the sound of this,
no, not a tiny bit,
He shuffled over to the bed
and on the edge did sit.

"I don't know what you mean.", said Jack
the boy was at a loss,
"I'm dying, son," said Pongo Foo,
"I'm off to see the Boss".
Now Pongo Foo was clever,
but he hadn't heard of tact,
And, if he had a failing,
it was subtlety he lacked.

"You're dying?" asked young Jack, aghast,
his voice approaching tears,
"Aye, lad, I am," said Pongo Foo,
"but let me calm your fears."
"I'm going to a better place,
with better silk for weaving,"
"And with a bit of practice,
who knows what I'll be achieving?"

"But we won't see you any more!"
Young Jack could only wail,
"What will we do for stories then?
Who else can spin a tale?"
"Now, lad, don't cry," said Pongo Foo,
"there's magic in this room",
"Everything will turn out fine,
there's no need for your gloom".

Jack wondered at old Pongo's words,
what did he have in mind?
When he was but a memory,
what would he leave behind?
Would Pongo's dreams fade gently,
or evaporate like dew,
Or would they somehow linger,
as the best ones sometimes do?

All this, of course, was overlaid
with thoughts of Pongo's fate,
The children couldn't cope, Jack knew,
they'd be in such a state,
For all adored the gaunt old man,
with eyes of emerald green,
Who took the night and made it theirs,
with every single dream.

When evening fell Jack had to leave
with tears in his eyes,
For he was just a boy
and not accustomed to goodbyes.
Then Pongo took him by the hand
and said "Don't fear, my lad!"
"You'll see old Pongo Foo again,
it's really not so bad!"

Jack left the cottage, wandered home
and settled into bed,
He couldn't sleep a wink
with all that worry in his head,
He tossed and turned throughout the night
and when the sun appeared,
He got straight up and wandered back
confronting what he feared

He walked straight through the door this time,
there was no point in knocking,
And when he got to Pongo's room
he noticed something shocking,
For Pongo Foo had left the scene,
no trace was to be found.
It seemed, for all the world,
that he'd been swallowed by the ground

But Pongo's chamber wasn't bare,
for right across the room,
There stretched the greatest dreaming web,
a thread-flower in bloom,
And in it's heart, a little weaver
worked at his display,
As if the world would stop
if there was ever a delay.

The little creature had eight legs;
a body, black and fuzzy,
He zipped across the structure,
oh, that little guy was busy!
Jack couldn't understand
what in the world was going on,
But Pongo'd had an inkling
what would happen when he'd gone.

His work was taken over
by these tiny, frantic weavers,
A merry band of skillful,
multi-legged over-achievers.
It came so naturally to
the little, fuzzy fellows,
(Though the one above old Pongo's bed
was puffing like a bellows.)

Poor Jack broke down in tears
upon the newly empty bed,
He didn't want this little beast,
he wanted Foo instead.
But as he lay there, wracked with grief,
he cried himself to sleep,
His sobs grew still as dreams began,
for now he needn't weep.

Old Pongo Foo was in his dream,
he strode about the place,
No longer bent and wrinkled,
with a smile upon his face,
"Look, boy, I told you! All is well!"
Foo bellowed with a grin,
"I'm in the pink! I'm chuffed to bits!
Look at the shape I'm in!"

"I'm working here, without a care,
in this, the dream dimension,"
"It's sunny and the sky is blue.
It's magic, did I mention?"
"The grass is greener over here,
the air a little sweeter,"
"And there's a charming little girl.
I hope some day you'll meet her."

"She brings me ale to ease my thirst,
and sits upon my knee"
"And when it's time for lunch,
she brings me sandwiches and tea"
Jack pondered this with growing doubt,
this couldn't be the truth,
Old Pongo had just died last night,
his eyes were ample proof.

"Dear Foo," Jack said, "how can it be,
that you've seen all this stuff?"
"For you've been here a night at most,
that's not nearly enough!"
"What's all this talk of sandwiches,
and sweeter air, and knees?"
"I don't believe a word of it,
don't patronise me, please!"

Foo smiled and shook his head,
"There's quite a bit that you don't know",
"Boy, when you dreamed my dreams at night,
where did you think I'd go?"
"I'm always with you in the dark,
to watch you through each night."
"For sometimes nightmares come along
and someone has to fight."

"I lived here in the night time,
just as you lived in the day."
"I've always lived in both, you see,
it was the only way,"
"To make sure that the dreams were safe,
and keep the kids from harm"
"And now I've died, I'm staying here,
in dreamland, in the warm."

Jack cried again, for different reasons,
Pongo understood,
He hugged the boy close to his chest
and squoze him well and good.
"I've got to go now", Pongo said,
"It's time for you to wake",
"Please take care of the spiders for me.
Promise, for my sake."

And so it came to pass
that spiders took up Pongo's mission,
For what else did you think it was
that wove with such precision?
So next time that you see a spider
crawling 'round your bath,
Don't squish him, help the poor chap out,
and spare yourself his wrath.

Who knows, a grateful spider
might decide to grant debentures,
And when you go to sleep,
perhaps he'll thrill you with adventures.
One thing's for certain, all agree,
that Pongo's little friends,
are story-weavers without peer,
and here our story ends.

So, that's the tale of Pongo Foo,
an odd, and lengthy poem,
And here begin the stories you can dream,
now that you know him,
For Pongo's spiders work in secret
all across the land,
And every night, while children sleep,
new dreams are being planned...

The Cautionary Tale of Oddly Wavering

The tale of Oddly Wavering
is not a happy story,
For Oddly was a kitchen boy
and destined not for glory,
He scrubbed at pitchers, chopping boards
and gleaming silver ladles,
And dreamed of knights and maidens
and the other stuff of fables.

His lot in life was simple
and he took it on the chin,
He'd scour the pots with fervour
and a merry little grin,
But when the dishes went away
in cupboards on the wall,
He'd spend his time lamenting
that it wasn't fair at all.

As time went by, young Oddly,
disenchanted with his lot,
Became a grumpy so and so,
the cleaning went to pot.
At 12 years old, the boy became
a stroppy, surly fellow,
And not at all like once he was,
so meek and kind and mellow.

He argued with the kitchen maids
and grumbled at the cook,
He bashed the pots and pans about,
he really pushed his luck,
One day the cook had had enough
and showed the boy the door,
And made it plain that Oddly
wasn't welcome anymore.

Oddly packed a little bag
and started on his journey,
He'd seek his fortune as a squire,
or tilting in the tourney,
It was the kitchen's loss, he knew,
it wasn't his concern,
They'd beg to have him back,
but Oddly vowed not to return.

He wandered out of town a ways,
intent to start his quest,
He might not be a valiant lad,
but Oddly'd do his best,
There must be someone out this way
who'd love to take him in,
A knight upon a charger,
so his training could begin.

Oddly wandered aimlessly,
with neither rhyme nor reason,
He strolled the countryside,
eating apples out of season,
He came upon a little bridge
above a gentle brook,
And stopped a while upon the bank,
abandoned and forsook.

He ventured to the water's edge
and peered under the bridge,
And spied a troll of knobbly green,
asleep upon a ridge,
Oddly tried to creep away,
but wasn't quick enough,
The troll awoke and spoke to Oddly,
grumpily and gruff.

"Who trespasses so boldly
underneath this bridge of mine?"
"I'll crunch his bones and drink his blood,
upon him I will dine!"
Oddly quaked and quivered,
for the troll was huge and scary,
His knobbled arms were massive
and his bumpy face was hairy.

The boy was running out of options
as the troll grew nearer,
He couldn't run, he couldn't speak,
but wanted nothing dearer,
Eventually, the trembling lad
began to find his voice,
He plucked his courage, took a breath
and gave the troll a choice.

"I'm just a boy, oh knobbly troll,
and not above a snack,"
"My bones are thin, my blood is weak
and meat I clearly lack."
"But over there on yonder plain
there stands a little town,"
"Where men grow fat and ladies fair,
and cattle plump and brown."

"If you would spare me, mighty troll,
I'll take you over there,"
"Where you can feast on proper meat
and not this meagre fare."
The troll considered long and hard
for he was hard of thinking,
and hadn't had a decent meal
or any blood for drinking.

Eventually the monster chose
and crossed to Oddly's side,
"Show me where my dinner is,
take me where they hide!"
Oddly grinned a wicked grin,
he'd gotten off for sure,
And never more would be abused,
what boy could ask for more?

He took the troll across the plain
to where the village stood,
The pair arrived near midnight,
when the pickings would be good.
The troll resolved to pick the people
carefully from bed,
and eat the frightened wretches whole,
beginning with the head.

Apparently a person
is a tender, juicy treat,
Our blood so thick and tasty,
and the sweetest, fatty meat.
The troll explained to Oddly
how a human skull would crunch,
The boy felt sickly all at once,
and nearly lost his lunch.

The scene was terrifying
as the troll began his feast,
He ate and ate until the sun
was rising in the East,
He ate the butcher and his wife
and ate the baker too,
And didn't spare the candlemaker
or his daughter, Sue.

Now this upset young Oddly
for the girl was quite a dish,
but he couldn't argue with the troll,
except to deeply wish:
"I wish I'd never met this beast,
I wish it very much!"
But the troll kept eating townspeople
and schoolchildren and such.

When all was done and all were dead
and chewed up in the troll,
The boy surveyed the carnage
and the vision took it's toll,
"I'm sorry," he wept, "I really am,
I didn't mean for this"
"I only wanted fun and freedom,
this is all amiss"

The troll regarded Oddly
with a greedy, nasty stare,
he put his arm around the boy
and ruffled up his hair,
he said "Now, boy, don't be so glum,
I hate to see you hurt"
"In fact, there's still a little space,
I'll eat you for dessert"

The boy submitted gladly
to his awful, crunchy fate,
He knew he was responsible
for what the monster ate,
"Eat me quickly then," he said,
"there's no point in delaying"
"Get it done with presently,
I can't abide your playing"

And so the troll ate Oddly
in a single, nasty gulp,
He crushed his bones between his teeth
and mashed him to a pulp,
The last thing Oddly thought
as he was chewed up into bits,
was how a boy should be aware
of where in life he fits.

For Oddly was a kitchen boy
and destined not for glory,
and had he stayed there
I would not be telling you this story,
No one would have had to fret
about the greedy troll,
And Oddly might have found his place
in life there, after all.

So don't be sad for Oddly,
for it really was his fault,
and tell yourself you'll never,
ever be quite such a dolt,
think carefully before you leap
and save yourself his fate,
for few endings are anywhere
as bad as being ate.

The Moon is Not Made of Cheese

In Donkeyfew in ages past
there was a mighty king,
Who had a purple castle,
oh it was a wondrous thing,
He had a score of servants
and a chamberlain or two,
A very merry monarch
was the king of Donkeyfew.

His name was Perivale and he was
known throughout the world,
For his scientific exploits,
his moustache and how it curled,
But mostly for the science,
for the king was quite a geek,
and used his skills to benefit
the downtrodden and meek.

But Perivale had one ambition,
greater than the rest,
There was a proposition
he was desperate to test,
The king was often smitten
with this wondering disease,
For he wanted to be certain
if the moon was made of cheese.

"For if it's made of cheese," he said,
"a wonder that would be"
"And we could mine for Camembert,
or Wensleydale for tea"
The king was most excited
by the question in his mind,
And decided to determine
what explorers he could find.

A man of courage, bravery,
but brains above all things
Would be required to reach the moon
and surf between its rings,
to find the surface, take a sample,
bring it safely home,
To good King Perivale
within his kingly, purple dome.

Such a man was Lickspittle,
a journeying mechanic,
Who studied motors, jets and things
until they made him manic,
His eyes were framed with goggles
and his face was black with soot,
but on the moon the king was sure
he'd know what was afoot.

So they built a mighty rocket
out of old tin baths and string,
and filled it up with fireworks,
nothing less would launch the thing,
it was a mighty vessel,
and it really looked the part,
but when they tried the engine,
it just sounded like a fart.

The king despaired and told Lickspittle,
"fix it if you can",
"I long to know about the moon,
and surely you're the man."
Lickspittle grinned and snapped his goggles
firmly into place,
and set to work immediately,
the grin still on his face.

He found the problem, sure enough,
within a week or two,
Too many baths there were, it seemed,
and fireworks too few.
They rigged it up with string again
as tight as it could be,
The strings were stretched,
but Perivale regarded it with glee.

"Will it fly this time, O, Lickspittle?
Please tell me that it will"
"For certain, sire," said Lickspittle,
his face was grinning still.
"There's half a ton of Catherine Wheels
and forty Roman Candles"
"I'll take her for a spin tonight
and see how well she handles"

The rocket was a big success,
it swooped across the skies,
and out into the blackness
where the moon sedately lies.
Lickspittle brought his craft about
and landed her back down,
on Donkeyfew's green meadows,
safely on the ground.

Next day Lickspittle marched to where
the vast machine was parked,
He bade farewell to Perivale,
and stepped into his ark,
He fired the engine, with a grin,
for such was his demeanour
And plunged off into space itself
in search of cheeses greener.

Perivale addressed the crowds
that gathered at the site,
"Dear friends and loyal subjects all,
I wonder if we might"
"find vintage cheddar, gorgonzola,
emmental and brie"
"Upon our lumpy satellite,
what wonders will we see?"

The crowd believed their king was barking,
mad as he could be,
but they suffered his long speeches
until it was time for tea,
Lickspittle, on the other hand,
was having quite a time,
the rocket surged beneath him
on it's steep and scary climb.

He circled round the planet twice,
to check the rocket's thrust,
For if it failed upon the moon
his luck he'd have to trust,
but all was fine and presently
he aimed towards the moon,
and marvelled at its surface,
knowing he'd be down there soon.

The rocket touched down gracefully,
upon the lunar surface,
Lickspittle donned a spacesuit
that'd he'd fashioned for the purpose,
and took a walk upon the moon,
his grin was still in place,
he'd made it to his target
through the emptiness of space.

He bounced around a little bit,
for such is protocol,
when you're a lunar vistor,
it doesn't do at all,
to walk like normal people,
for then what would be the fun,
of being on the moon, you see,
it really isn't done.

He tired of bouncing presently,
and fetched a little pot,
he picked up samples with a pair
of tweezers that he'd got,
from Perivale's palace,
from a silver sugar bowl,
one sample caught his eye,
and he resolved to eat it whole.

Now, this is not the brightest move
the man will ever make,
but it's vital to our story,
and so for the story's sake,
Lickspittle took a mighty bite,
his eyes went very wide,
"The moon's not made of cheese at all!",
the poor mechanic cried.

He took his samples to the ship,
his mind was all a fluster,
He pushed the rocket home
with all the courage he could muster,
For Perivale would not be pleased
to learn his tale of woe,
Lickspittle wondered if to prison
shortly he would go.

For failing kings is not something
a person lightly does,
the thrill of bearing bad news
is an overrated buzz,
Lickspittle fretted constantly
until he reached the planet,
and parked the ship upon a nearby
mountainside of granite.

He kept the vessel close at hand
in case escape was needed,
The king was not a nasty man,
but common sense he heeded,
it isn't prudent to provide
yourself with no escape,
When dealing with a monarch
who might soon be going ape.

Our explorer reached the palace
and approached the throne in fear,
and wondered if this setback
was about to cost him dear,
Perivale reclined upon
his throne of solid gold,
and clapped his hands anticipating
tales he'd soon be told.

Lickspittle cleared his throat
and simply offered up the pot,
His face was beetroot purple
and his cheeks were getting hot.
"Sire," he said, "I'm sorry,
but the moon's not made of cheese"
"It's something different altogether,
try it if you please"

Perivale took the little pot
and peered under the lid,
to see what curious substances
beneath the rim were hid,
He took a taste, and suddenly
the king could only beam,
"The moon's not made of cheese,
it's made of butterscotch ice cream!"

So, Lickspittle was knighted
and acquired a new commission,
For forthright action, derring do,
and flying with precision,
He got a silver medal,
and a costly golden watch,
As master of the King's ice cream,
(in brackets, butterscotch).

Printed in the United Kingdom
by Lightning Source UK Ltd.
121518UK00002B/320/A